VICTOR STOPS THE SCHOOL BULLY

**Keith Vitali
and Sam Oates**

Foreword by: Dr. José Luis Hinojosa

Illustrated by: Joe Byrne

www.KeithVitaliEnterprises.com
k1vitali@gmail.com
PO Box 768741
Roswell GA 30076

ISBN: 978-0-692-93111-0

Cataloging in Publication Data is on file at the Library of Congress

Vitali, Keith and Oates, Sam
Victor Stops the School Bully/Keith Vitali and Sam Oates
Juvenile – Fiction

Summary: "Victor Stops the School Bully," is a book dealing with issues that so many kids experience when moving to a new school. Victor is a 10-year old boy who is nervous about such a move. Guided by Mr. Mike, his karate instructor, and his training, Victor deals with his new teacher, his new classmates, issues with honesty and integrity, and learns how to handle the school bully.

Printed in the United States of America

ACKNOWLEDGMENTS

A special thanks to Dr. José Luis Hinojosa, Sharon Finney, and Keith Strandberg for help with this book.

I want to thank my loving grandson, Sam, for not only inspiring me to write this book but for helping me write it from his 10-year-old perspective. Sam, just like Victor, felt nervous and self-conscious about having to move to a new school in the third grade.

A special thank you goes to my caring and beautiful wife, Kathy, for her love and friendship, our incredible kids, Jennifer, Kristen, and Travis, along with my precious granddaughter, Alma Rose.

Just like Victor and Sam, I moved to a new school in the third grade and had to deal with the same fears and anxieties. A special thank you goes out to my own third-grade teacher, Mrs. Robinson, whose care, and kindness, impacted my entire life in such a positive manner.

I want to thank my good friend, Mike Genova, on whom I based the instructor, guiding Victor in the book. Mike is one of the most knowledgeable and talented Martial Arts instructors in America and I personally want to thank him for his lifetime commitment to teaching children.

INTRODUCTION

Hi, my name is Keith Vitali. I wrote this illustrated children's book because, as a parent and grandparent, I know what it's like to send a child off to school with all their hopes and dreams in front of them, knowing full well how unsure they are about this new adventure in life.

With my lifelong experience as a martial arts instructor, competitor, writer, actor, and producer, I believe I can teach young readers and their parents how to deal with issues that so many kids experience when moving to a new school and making new friends.

And of course, bullying issues are always at the back of every child's and parent's mind, so the learning methods and strategies in this book on how to deal with bullies are invaluable.

I am also pleased to co-author this book with my grandson, Sam, utilizing his own personal anecdotes, his fears, and anxieties that he too felt when he first moved to his new school.

We hope that you enjoy the book!

FOREWORD

For many children, the thought of starting school can be a frightening experience. School-age children will face a series of challenges, many times for the first time in their lives - and Mommy and Daddy will probably not be there to help. Some of these stress-provoking challenges are: 1) making a good first impression – body language is important. 2) taking a test - add another dose of stress if someone is trying to copy from you. 3) doing the right thing – it takes personal discipline to do the right thing. And 4) bullying – what is bullying anyway?

Bullying is defined as a form of aggression in which 1) the behavior is intended to harm or disturb. 2) the behavior occurs repeatedly over time, and 3) there is a difference and imbalance in power, with a more powerful person (or group) attacking a less powerful one. The difference in power may be physical, or psychological.

Examples of: Verbal bullying – name-calling and threats. Physical bullying – hitting. Psychological bullying – rumors, shunning, or exclusion.

"Serious attention" and "preventive intervention" are what my good friend, Keith Vitali, world-renowned children's self-defense expert and world championship martial artist, addresses in "Stopping the School Bully." He tackles the school challenges I mentioned above in true championship fashion. Keith describes, in an easy-to-read approach, some possible solutions to problems associated with everyday school life.

Because of the timeless nature and importance of the subject matter, I would encourage parents to sit down and read this book with their children. Besides being a great bonding opportunity, it will be also a great learning experience for everyone. I am confident the information found in "Stop the School Bully" will teach your child some valuable lessons not only for school but for life.

José Luis Hinojosa, MD, MHA, American Board of Family Practice Diplomate, American Academy of Pain Management
715 Sunrise Ave
Oakley, Kansas 67748
BooksByDrHinojosa.com

Victor just passed his test at
his karate school

"Congratulations, you have just earned your
GOLD BELT," said Mr. Mike.

"Wow! I've only been taking karate for three months
and getting promoted to gold belt feels so, so,
AWESOME," replied Victor.

"Victor, you should be very proud of yourself
because of how hard you've worked in class.
Keep up the good work and before too long, you will
become a black belt," said Mr. Mike.

"I hope so, but right now I'm really worried
about attending a new school and surviving the
third grade," replied Victor.

"You can do anything when you put your mind to it,
Victor," said Mr. Mike. "You just proved it earning
your gold belt. I want you to apply that same
positive attitude in your new school."

"On your first day of school, I want you to do
your best to smile and make new friends.

Remember, most of the other kids at school are just as nervous as you are," replied Mr. Mike.

"Just be yourself and you will do just fine," said Mr. Mike.

"I hope Mr. Mike is right," thought Victor. "So, this is Bradley Elementary School. It's so BIG and look at all those kids," thought Victor.

"Mr. Mike said to just BE MYSELF... but what if they don't like who I am?" thought Victor.

"I also heard that there is a BULLY in every class. Oh no! What if the bully doesn't like the way I LOOK or TALK or DRESS?" thought Victor.

Victor snapped out of that way of thinking and remembered what Mr. Mike had taught him.

"Ok Victor, you can do this," thought Victor and before he knew it, he had walked all the way into his classroom.

"Just my luck, I'm the first one in class," thought Victor.

Victor was wrong though; there was another person in the room.

His new teacher!

"Oh geez, by the looks of this teacher, this school year is going to be so hard. She looks **TOUGH,**" thought Victor.

Victor realized he was being silly and was just nervous about meeting her.

"The best thing to do when meeting someone if you're nervous is to just to say hi," remembered Victor.

Victor remembered if you want to make a good first impression, you should give a firm handshake, look them in the eye and be sure to smile.

Victor put on an ear-to-ear grin and walked right up to his teacher and stuck out his hand.

"Hi, my name is Victor," said Victor making sure he looked her straight in her eyes as he spoke.

"Nice to meet you, Victor, my name is Mrs. Robinson," said Mrs. Robinson. "That's some handshake you have."

"Thanks," said Victor. "Nice to meet you too, Mrs. Robinson."

Victor walked back to his desk and could not stop grinning.

"Good morning class, my name is
Mrs. Robinson," said Mrs. Robinson.

"Hi, Mrs. Robinson," the entire class responded.

"First, I want to learn more about each of you.
Please come up to the front of the class and tell me a
little bit about yourselves," said Mrs. Robinson.

"Victor, why don't you go first?" said Mrs.
Robinson.

Victor felt his stomach hurting, the air
creeping out of his lungs, his knees felt weak
and he started feeling nervous again.

"I hope I don't stutter. I would hate it if
everyone laughed at me.

I'm so nervous," thought Victor.

"Mr. Mike said to take a big breath and do your best to relax. Stand up straight and try not to fidget moving around so much and speak up so everyone can hear you," remembered Victor.

"Sounds easy enough, but why am I so nervous?" thought Victor.

"Yes Ma'am," Victor replied nervously as he walked to the front of the room.

Victor saw Mrs. Robinson smiling at him.

"Hi, my name is Victor and I'm 10-years old," said Victor to the class.

"I love sports. My favorite sports are lacrosse, basketball, baseball, swimming, skiing, and I also like to scooter and, oh yeah, I also take karate and just earned my gold belt," beamed Victor.

"I also love spaghetti and meatballs, and pizza. Oh, how I love pizza," said Victor.

"Oh, oh! Who's that big guy in the back of the class?" thought Victor.

It was Byron. Kids called him Byron the bully.

"One time, Byron gave another kid a swirly at school and that he made his teachers do his homework," thought Victor.

Victor felt the air creeping out of his lungs again.

"The best way to deal with bullies is to try and make them your friend," remembered Victor.

"Right now, I've better finish talking to the class," thought Victor.

"I also like to snowboard, throw a football and play soccer," concluded Victor.

"That will be enough for now. Wow, Victor, you really like sports, don't you?" said Mrs. Robinson.

"One more thing, I also love to throw meatballs at my dad," replied Victor. "One time I hit my dad with a meatball from across the room and..."

The entire classroom started to laugh.
"Okay Victor, you can take your seat now," giggled Mrs. Robinson.

As the class settled down, Victor thought he even saw Byron smile, but it might have been his imagination.

"Cool, not bad the first time out," thought Victor.
"Well, Victor, that was very... entertaining," said Mrs. Robinson.

"Okay, class let's go outside and take a quick recess," said Mrs. Robinson.

As Victor walked to recess, a classmate named Billy tapped him on the shoulder.

"Hey Victor, look what I have," said Billy, "I found this watch on the floor."

"Cool, whose is it?" asked Victor.

"I don't know, but it's mine now," replied Billy, "Finders keepers."

"That sure is a nice watch and Billy didn't steal it, he just found it, but it still doesn't seem right," thought Victor.

Then Victor remembered Mr. Mike's school creed, about integrity and honesty. "I guess this must have been what he was talking about."

"Billy, what if the watch belongs to someone else and they're looking for it?" said Victor. "Shouldn't you give it to Mrs. Robinson and see if someone has lost it?"

"You're right," replied Billy, "I didn't really think about that."

When Victor and Billy got back to class, Billy handed the watch to Mrs. Robinson.

"Here, Mrs. Robinson," said Billy, "I found this in the hallway."

Mrs. Robinson's eyes lit up as she said, "Oh, thank you, Billy, this watch is very special to me. I must have accidentally dropped it."

Mrs. Robinson gave Billy a big hug and Victor was proud of his new friend.

Mrs. Robinson moved to the front of the room, "Ok, class, now that you are all back from recess, we're going to take a short math quiz. No pressure, boys, and girls. I just want to see where you are at this stage, that's all," said Mrs. Robinson.

Victor pulled out a freshly sharpened pencil and began his quiz.

3 x 3 = 9.

4 x 4 = 16. "Sixteen, when I turn sixteen, I'm going to get a super-fast car," thought Victor.

"Oh no," thought Victor, "I've got to focus like Mr. Mike said when taking a test and get my mind back on what I'm doing."
Victor took a deep breath and continued.

5 x 5 = Victor noticed the boy beside him was looking at his paper.

"Shouldn't he be doing his own work?" thought Victor.

It was the first day of school and Victor wanted to make friends, but not by letting them cheat off his paper.

As he covered up his answers, Victor remembered what Mr. Mike had said about honesty:

"Always be honest and tell the truth."

"Ok, class, times up!" said Mrs. Robinson

"I think I did pretty good on the quiz," thought Victor. "Mr. Mike would also be proud of how I didn't let that boy copy my answers."

"Here comes that boy that tried to copy from me. I hope he's not mad," thought a worried, Victor.

"Hi! My name is Tommy," said Tommy.

"Hi Tommy," replied Victor. "Sorry about not letting you copy my test, but I didn't think it was right."

"It's Ok, Victor," said Tommy. "I'm sorry and hope you're not mad at me."

"Forget it, Tommy," said Victor.

Victor and Tommy were in the lunchroom line
when Tommy spotted Byron the Bully. "Oh no,
here comes Byron," said Tommy.

Victor knew that he had to make a good first
impression if he was going to make friends with
Byron, this was his best chance.

Victor tried his best to stand up straight and
smile as he noticed Tommy trying to sneak away.

Byron noticed it too
and grabbed
Tommy's cake
before he could run
away.

"Hey kid," said Byron. "I'll take that." Byron stuffed the entire piece of cake in his mouth in one bite.

"That's my cake," said Tommy.

"What are you going to do about it, wimp?" said Byron with a mouthful of cake.

"Well, nothing," said Tommy, sadly.

Victor thought Byron was not nice for taking Tommy's cake, but maybe he was just hungry and did not know any better.

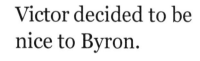

Victor decided to be nice to Byron.

"Hey, that was cool stuffing that whole cake in your mouth in one bite, I've never seen anything like that before," said Victor.

"It was?" said a confused Byron.
"It was?" added a surprised Tommy.

"I wish I could do that. Hey, I have an idea. My Mom's baking a cake for me and some of my friends after school today. Why don't you come over and show me how you did that?" asked Victor.

"Me?" replied Byron.
"Yeah sure, and then we can play basketball later," said Victor. "Tommy can come too."

"I love basketball," stuttered Byron. "I guess I'll see you after school then."

"Ok, see you then," said Victor.

"Umm, I'm sorry I took your cake, Tommy," muttered Byron, "I hope you can come to play basketball with us this afternoon."

"It's ok, I don't like strawberry cake anyway," said Tommy.

"I can't believe Byron is being so nice – he's even high-fiving me," thought Victor. "Mr. Mike was right. Most bullies are just looking for a friend. Even a hungry bully like Byron!"

Victor could not believe it. His first day of school was almost over and he had already made three new friends.

He could not wait to tell his Mom and Dad.

"Hey, Mom, hey, Dad," said Victor as he came in the door.

"How was your first day of school?" asked Victor's Mom.

"It was great," replied Victor, "I've already made three new friends and I've invited them over to play. Is that OK?"

"That's fine, Victor," replied Victor's Mom, "But be sure to get your homework done first."

"Remember, Victor," said Victor's Dad, "Your Mom and I have our responsibilities...and your responsibility is to do your homework."

"Ok, Dad" said Victor, "I'll do it right now."

"Mr. Mike would be so proud of me," thought Victor, "I can't wait for my next karate class."

The End.

Dealing with Bullies

Verbal abuse, name-calling and saying hurtful things is a form of bullying also. This type of bullying many times inflicts more pain and damage than a physical assault. Verbal abuse can often cause a child to remember those damaging insults for the rest of their lives.

Another form of bullying is associated with exclusion. Not allowing others to join in or having little "cliques" where only certain "cool" friends can hang out together.

Here are ten other tips for you if you are being bullied at school. Mr. Mike says that we should practice these tips at home with our parents.

Dealing with Bullies

1. Nine out of ten times, a bully is someone you know, a friend, a classmate, someone you play with at the park, or perhaps, even a brother or sister. So, we just do not want to strike back at the bully who might not even be aware they are bullying.

2. Tell someone if you are being bullied – tell someone you trust, like your parents or your teacher.

3. Walk away – Always tries to avoid a fight, especially when the bully might be a brother or sister.

4. Try treating the bully as a friend instead of an enemy--like Victor did with Byron.

5. Smile and project a confident personality – a scary situation can turn into a funny one if you use your head. But never make fun of a bully.

6. Project a look of confidence with body language– For example, look in the mirror and try to appear as weak and meek as possible with the way you

stand. This is the look the bully is drawn to. Next, this time stand up straight and strong working on projecting a look of confidence.

7. Project a look of confidence with facial expressions. First, stand in front of the mirror and look as scared and meek as you can. Again, this look of fear and meekness is what the bully is drawn to. Next, begin working on projecting a powerful, confident look with your facial expressions.

8. Focus on subjects that the bully might enjoy, such as sports, movies, or music, for example. Attempt to engage them in things they care about.

9. Sometimes standing up to a bully is the only solution to stop the continued bullying and I stress you to be careful here, use words and body language to say NO to a bully.

10. And finally, like Mr. Mike said, smile and just be yourself and tell the bully that they are bullying. Sometimes, they are not aware they're bullying in the first place.

About the Authors

Keith Vitali is a 10th-degree black belt and a leading expert on children's safety. Keith is a three-time former national martial arts champion and was elected into *Black Belt Magazine's* prestigious **Black Belt Hall of Fame.** Keith is also considered one of the top ten fighters of all time according to *Black Belt Magazine.* Keith's national martial arts exposure led him to star in a series of action movies including "Revenge of the Ninja" and "Wheels on Meals" with Jackie Chan.

Keith Vitali is also a published author, penning four instructional how-to martial arts books as well as a successful children's video, "Self Defense for Kids," that dealt with bullying issues.

Oprah introduced Keith on her show as one of the premier experts on children's safety and Keith has been featured on the front page of USA Today as well as every nationally syndicated newspaper in America. Currently, Keith is focusing on children's issues dealing with bullying.

Sam Oates is an avid sports lover and assisted in writing this book. His unique personal perspective with anxieties and fears like millions of other kids his age entering a new school dealing with bullying issues was instrumental in influencing the writing of this book.

Mike Genova and Keith Vitali

www.KeithVitaliEnterprises.com

My good friend, **Mike Genova**, on whom I based the instructor in this book guiding Victor, is one of the leading children's martial arts experts in the United States. Mike is a former top-ten national tournament fighter and owns one of the most successful karate schools in South Carolina where he has been teaching for over 40 years.

Mike is pictured with his beautiful wife, Shelley, being presented the Order of the Silver Crescent Award by Nikki Haley, the former governor of South Carolina and Ambassador to the United Nations. Mike was also presented the Order of the Palmetto Award by South Carolina governor, Henry McMaster – both awards are the two highest civilian awards in South Carolina for community service. Mike is also the President of the South Carolina Black Belt Hall of Fame.

Mike Genova can be contacted at:
130 C Pontiac Business Center Drive Elgin SC, 29045 – Genovafamilykarate.com